Highlights **Puzzle Readers**

LEVEL **P**

LET'S DISCOVER READING

Bear and Friends

Pup Is Lost

By Jody Jensen Shaffer
Art by Clair Rossiter

HIGHLIGHTS PRESS

Honesdale, Pennsylvania

Stories + Puzzles = Reading Success!

Dear Parents,

Highlights Puzzle Readers are an innovative approach to learning to read that combines puzzles and stories to build motivated, confident readers.

Developed in collaboration with reading experts, the stories and puzzles are seamlessly integrated so that readers are encouraged to read the story, solve the puzzles, and then read the story again. This helps increase vocabulary and reading fluency and creates a satisfying reading experience for any kind of learner. In addition, solving puzzles fosters important reading and learning skills such as:

- shape and letter recognition
- letter-sound relationships
- visual discrimination
- logic
- flexible thinking
- sequencing

With high-interest stories, humorous characters, and trademark puzzles, Highlights Puzzle Readers offer a winning combination for inspiring young learners to love reading.

These are Bear's friends.

This is Bear.

This is Mouse.

This is Fox.

This is Squirrel.

This is Pup.

Help Fox and his friends look for **Pup**.

Then find the letter **P** hidden in each picture of this story.

Are you there?

Happy reading!

7

Are you here?

16

17

Fox found Pup! But something else was hiding. Did you find the letter **P** hidden in each picture of this story? Now match each **P** word below with its picture.

Pup

Pie

Pot

For information about permission to reprint selections from this book, please contact permissions@highlights.com.

Published by Highlights Press
815 Church Street
Honesdale, Pennsylvania 18431
ISBN (paperback): 978-1-64472-682-2
ISBN (hardcover): 978-1-64472-683-9
ISBN (ebook): 978-1-64472-684-6
Library of Congress Control Number: 2021950471
Manufactured in Melrose Park, IL, USA
Mfg. 01/2022
First edition
Visit our website at Highlights.com.
10 9 8 7 6 5 4 3 2 1

This book has been officially leveled by using the F&P Text Level Gradient™ Leveling System.

CERTIFIED LEXILE PARTNER

LEXILE®, LEXILE FRAMEWORK®, LEXILE ANALYZER®, the LEXILE® logo and POWERV® are trademarks of MetaMetrics, Inc., and are registered in the United States and abroad. The trademarks and names of other companies and products mentioned herein are the property of their respective owners. Copyright © 2021 MetaMetrics, Inc. All rights reserved.

For assistance in the preparation of this book, the editors would like to thank Julie Tyson, MSEd Reading, MSEd Administration K–12, Title 1 Reading Specialist; and Gina Shaw.